The Shadow Nose

The Shadow Nose

by ELIZABETH LEVY

illustrated by MORDICAI GERSTEIN

cover by Tricia Zimic

SCHOLASTIC INC.

New York Toronto London Auckland Sydney Tokyo

ISBN 0-590-33281-3
Reading level is determined by using the Spache Readibility Formula.
2.2 signifies high second grade level.

Text copyright © 1983 by Elizabeth Levy.
Illustrations copyright © 1983 by Mordicai Gerstein.
All rights reserved.
This edition published by Scholastic Inc.,
730 Broadway, New York, NY 10003,
by arrangement with William Morrow & Company.

12 11 10 9 8 7 6 5 4 3   6 7 8 9 / 8 0/9

Printed in the U.S.A.   28

To Dana and Erica,
with love

Contents

A Shadow on a Drizzly Day

My name is Lamont. I'm named after a character in an old radio show, Lamont Cranston. He was The Shadow. My parents tell me that The Shadow could make himself invisible. The Shadow always knew what evil lurked in men's hearts. I don't know much about evil, but I do know you shouldn't give your kid a weird name. Believe me, in the year 2000, nobody is going to want to be called Mork.

Diana, my sister, is named after Wonder Woman, but she's no Amazon. She's a shrimp. I call her Wonder Shrimp. She doesn't have the wisdom of Athena, the strength of Hercules, or the speed of Mercury. Well, maybe the speed. For a shrimp, she can move fast, especially on the basketball court.

Diana is in the third grade. I'm in the fifth. We go to the Little Red Schoolhouse in the Greenwich Village part of New York City. My dad is an artist. He works at home in our apartment in a brownstone that was built before the Revolutionary War. We pay a lot of rent for a place where the floors slant and the walls sag and crack. It's supposed to be quaint. My mom is always getting involved with groups that want to keep the neighborhood just the way it is.

My story begins on a drizzly April day. Diana and I were walking home from school when we stopped to watch a basketball game in the playground around the corner from our school. A crowd had gathered even though it was so wet.

Some of the best basketball players in the city hang out in the playgrounds of Greenwich Village. The players are mostly grown-ups or teenagers, and they play for money.

Wily Will is my favorite player. He's big, and you wouldn't think he'd be fast, but, oh boy, is he quick. He's out there hustling all the time. Wily Will winked at me through the chain link fence. He noticed me watching him. Wily Will notices everything. He always plays partners with Swivel Hips George. Swivel Hips is a tough player. He elbows under the boards, and he shouts and yells a lot. Nobody likes to call a foul on Swivel Hips.

I was watching Wily Will dart all over the court when I saw something so strange that I did a double take. Wily Will went up for a lay-up. His shadow didn't.

"Diana, look at Wily Will's shadow," I said.

"Who cares about his shadow," said Diana. "Boy, would I like to have his moves."

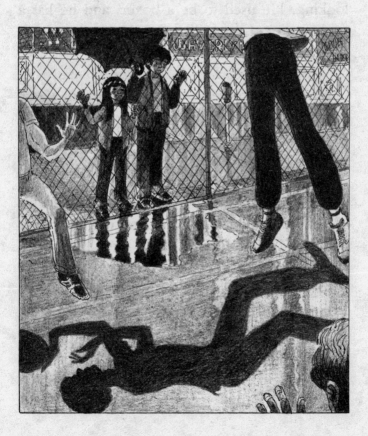

"That's just it. His shadow doesn't move. Look, it's painted on the basketball court." I pointed. Wily Will's profile was painted on the center of the court in a ghostly pearly grey paint. It looked just like a shadow, but on a drizzly day it was the only shadow in sight.

Wily Will took a break and came and leaned against the fence near us. He wiped the sweat off his forehead. He's about six foot three and tough looking. He used to be a boxer, and he has a broken nose. It looks like a potato that someone started to mash.

"Good moves, Wily Will," said Diana.

Wily Will accepted Diana's compliment with a nod. "I'm gonna win myself fifty dollars today." I bet that Wily Will makes almost as much as professional basketball players just by hustling games at the playground.

"Lamont is always trying to copy your tricks, Wily Will," said Diana. "Lamont tries to dribble between his legs like you do . . . and behind his back."

"Sneaky, huh," said Wily Will. "Hey, Swivel Hips, hey guys . . . this here is Lamont!"

"Ha, so what?" asked Swivel Hips. He starts most sentences with the word "ha." Wily Will led me into the playground. Diana followed us.

We stood right next to his shadow painted on the court.

All the guys crowded around us. Diana grabbed my hand. "What do you want with me?" I asked, trying to keep my voice from shaking.

"Lamont was the real name of The Shadow on that old radio show," said Wily Will.

"Ha, I didn't know that," said Swivel Hips. Swivel Hips turned to me. "Will has been acting spooked all day, ever since he found his shadow fixed to the ground." Swivel Hips laughed.

"It's no laughing matter," said Wily Will. "I don't like anyone messing with my image."

"I didn't paint it," I said.

"Yeah," said Diana. "You can't accuse him just 'cause his name's Lamont, and 'cause he's a good artist like our dad."

I wished she had kept her trap shut. "Your dad's an artist, huh?" said Wily Will.

"I never saw this shadow before in my life," I said. "I can't paint this good."

Wily Will narrowed his eyes at me. "The Shadow knows . . . doesn't he?"

"I don't know a thing," I whispered.

Wily Will glared. "The Shadow knows. . . ."

2

Don't Go Down

"Did you paint that shadow?" Diana asked after we got out of the playground.

"No," I groaned.

"Well, you could have. Everyone says that you've got Dad's talent."

"Watch where you're walking," I said to change the subject. Diana was wearing her Miss Piggy pink satin running shoes, and she was ruining them sloshing through puddles.

Suddenly I stopped. We were right in front of Zylber's Butcher Shop on Bleecker Street. I saw an outline of a grey leg shimmering underneath the puddle.

"What the . . . !" I exclaimed. "Another one!" This one had a fat belly. It looked very familiar. Then it hit me. It looked exactly like Mr. Zylber.

Just then Mr. Zylber himself appeared outside his shop, followed by Mr. Mosconi, the owner of our favorite Italian restaurant.

"See," said Mr. Zylber, pointing to his shadow. "It just appeared in the middle of the night."

Mr. Mosconi chuckled, "It looks just like you, belly and all."

Mr. Zylber groaned. He looked down at his own belly and then at the belly of the shadow. "I'm not that fat."

Mr. Mosconi patted Mr. Zylber's belly. "That's you all right. What did you do, decide that your belly was a good advertisement for your meat?" Mr. Mosconi poked Mr. Zylber in the belly again. Mr. Zylber didn't seem to find him funny. I was glad. I didn't find it funny either.

Mr. Zylber noticed Diana and me. He knows me because I do a lot of the shopping for our family. "Lamont, do you know anything about this?"

I shook my head.

"There's one on the playground, too," said Diana. "All the guys think Lamont did it."

Sometimes I wish Diana didn't have such an easy time talking to strangers.

"Lamont!" exclaimed Mr. Mosconi. "Of

course, Lamont Cranston, The Shadow. The Shadow knows everything."

"My name is Lamont Shapiro," I said. "And I *didn't* paint the shadow."

Mr. Mosconi winked at me. I didn't like his wink. It gave me a very uneasy feeling in the pit of my stomach.

"Let's go, Diana."

"This is weird," said Diana as we walked away. "How many of those shadow paintings did you do?"

"Cut it out," I snapped. "I didn't do them."

We passed the bag lady who lives on the corner by the subway station on 8th Street and Sixth Avenue. Everything she owns is in a shopping cart. Whenever you pass her, she always says, "Don't go down, don't go down." She even says that when you're not heading for the subway. Nobody knows her name. We just call her the Don't Go Down Lady.

Today she was crying. Tears hung on her cheeks. Nobody seemed to notice. People streamed by her into the subway station. Nobody stopped just because an old lady was crying.

I had to stop. "What's wrong?" I asked.

She looked up at me. I had never looked into her eyes before. They were blue, a cloudy blue.

Her skin was tough and leathery with red lines crisscrossing at the sides of her nose.

"Let's go," whispered Diana. "She's scary."

I knew she was scary, but she was also crying. "What's wrong?" I asked again.

The Don't Go Down Lady grabbed my arm above my elbow. She was much stronger than she looked. "Voodoo . . . evil," she whispered. She pointed to the wall beside her.

I should have guessed. The shadow artist had painted her shopping cart. "Somebody wants my spot," she whispered. "Somebody wants me to move."

"No, no," I said, but I knew nothing I could say would stop her tears. Diana pulled at my free arm. A train rumbled underground. When I was little, I used to think the sound of the subway was the earth breathing.

"Don't go down," whispered the shopping cart lady to me. She turned away. "Don't go down," she repeated to a man hurrying down the subway steps.

"Let's get out of here," said Diana.

We walked away. "Wait till I tell the kids at school that she grabbed you," said Diana. "I think she's a witch."

"She is not. She's a sad, scared lady."

"Maybe that shadow painting is a hex sign.

Maybe it means death." She said it in her best horror movie voice. Diana loves to go to horror movies, the creepier the better. I hate them.

"Will you shut up," I said. We turned the corner onto Jones Street, our block. A shadow fell across our stoop. I rubbed my eyes. I would have recognized that shadow anywhere. It was mine! You could see my curly hair and the bump on my nose.

Suddenly I knew how Wily Will, Mr. Zylber and the Don't Go Down Lady felt. Someone had been studying me when I wasn't looking. Somebody knew me so well that they could draw me from memory.

"It's you," whispered Diana. "Wow! What did you ever do to deserve this?"

It was a good question.

3

Reward

Shadow paintings turned up all over the Village. My father thought the artist had real talent. My mom wasn't so sure. She told me that the shadow epidemic was going to be discussed at the next community board meeting. I told her I wanted to be there.

On the night of the meeting, we left Diana at home with a baby-sitter. Boy, was I glad. We stopped for pizza at Famous Ray's on Sixth Avenue and Eleventh Street. It's the best there is. But I wasn't hungry. I was worried.

"What's wrong?" asked my father. He knew that normally I loved pizza with pepperoni.

"All the kids in school think I'm the one who is doing the shadow paintings."

My mother gave me a look of warning. "Lamont, if I go into that meeting tonight, and the artist turns out to be my own son. . . ."

"Ma, I'm innocent," I said. "Dad's the artist in this family."

My mother turned to my father. "You haven't been doing those paintings, have you?"

My father laughed. "Come on, you know I'm working hard for my show in June. But I do admire the artist. I wouldn't mind if it *was* Lamont."

Just then a hand grabbed the back of my neck. A voice hissed, "Lamont!" It was Mr. Zylber. I thought he was going to lift me off the ground. I could see the whites all around his eyes.

"Mr. Zylber," cried my mother. "What's wrong?"

"The Shadow knows what's wrong," he hissed. "I've had enough. It's not a joke anymore." He glared at Mom and Dad.

My father stood up. "Mr. Zylber, you have no right to speak to Lamont like that."

"Ha!" snorted Mr. Zylber, but he let me go and walked away.

"It's the shadow paintings," I said. "If you hadn't named me Lamont, I wouldn't be having all these problems."

"Lamont is a beautiful name," said my mother.

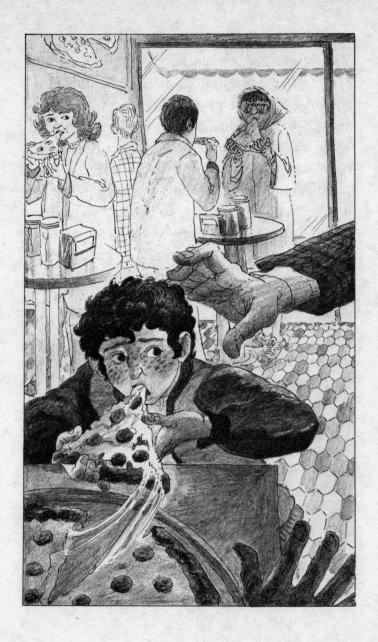

"You'd better not call me that at the meeting. You might get me lynched." I wasn't kidding. Mr. Zylber had been so angry it scared me. I couldn't understand it. He hadn't been that angry when the shadow painting first appeared. Why was he so upset now? Maybe Diana was right about the shadows being a hex.

The community meeting was held in the Jefferson Market Library on Sixth Avenue and Eighth Street. The library was built in the nineteenth century. It has towers and gargoyles on the outside, and a great curved staircase on the inside.

When we got to the library, it was almost packed. Mom went up to the front because she was one of the people in charge. Dad and I sat near the back.

I looked around. Ms. Bases was at the door, asking people to sign in. She owns Bases Antique Store on MacDougal Street. She makes her profit off tourists who come to the Village looking for bargains. She is seventy-six years old, and she likes to jog around Washington Square Park, which is a half mile around. She runs *really* slow. In fact, it's hard to tell that she's not walking. But someone once wrote an article about her as one of our "Village characters." She keeps a framed

copy of the article in her window to attract tourists.

Now she, too, has a shadow painting. It starts
with her sneakered feet and then snakes up the
wall. Part of her torso is painted on the glass of
her antique store. She doesn't mind. The tourists
love it, so it is okay with her.

She comes to all the community board meetings. She and my mom are friends. She always sits by the door and asks people to sign in.

Suddenly I heard Ms. Bases raise her voice. The Don't Go Down Lady was trying to come into the meeting with her shopping cart.

"I'm sorry," said Ms. Bases. "You can't bring that in here."

The Don't Go Down Lady tried to roll her shopping cart right over Ms. Bases' sneakered foot. "You have to let me in," she argued. "I know you are going to talk about those shadow paintings. I got a lot to say. And I can't leave my cart outside, it could be stolen. Besides, this cart is famous. It's now a painting."

That was the longest speech I had ever heard her make. I could understand why she wouldn't want to leave her cart outside. All she owned was in that cart. She didn't have a home.

"Dad," I whispered, nudging him. "Can you do something? I think they're going to kick out the Don't Go Down Lady."

My dad got up and whispered in Ms. Bases' ear. Whatever he said must have worked. The Don't Go Down Lady wheeled her cart into the room and down to the front row.

The meeting started. They went through the

boring old business first, the treasurer's report, complaints about landlords, complaints about loud music, a motion to plant more trees. Finally they got around to the shadow paintings.

"They're ugly," shouted Mr. Zylber. "They're the work of a sick mind!"

Other people in the audience started yelling too.

My mother pounded the gavel. "Has anyone ever seen the shadow artist?" she asked.

I twisted around in my seat. Wily Will caught me staring at him and winked at me.

I felt sure the artist was in the room. I wondered who it could be.

My dad? Could he have done it? He certainly had the talent. And my dad always likes a good joke.

Mr. Zylber? Why was he acting so strange?

Wily Will? Who knew what Wily Will was up to? Could the shadow paintings be some kind of new hustle?

The Don't Go Down Lady? Could she be an artist in disguise? She lived on the street. Could she go around in the middle of the night and do the paintings?

I jotted down my thoughts in a notebook. I get bored in meetings. I'm a lot like my father in that way.

I started to doodle. I sketched each of my suspects. I drew Wily Will with his broken nose and his muscular legs. I drew Ms. Bases with her gray hair and skinny legs. Mr. Zylber with his belly. The Don't Go Down Lady and her cart. I was so busy I forgot about the meeting.

Then I heard Mr. Zylber's booming voice. "I call for a vote on a hundred dollar reward for catching the shadow artist."

"I won't pay a penny," said Ms. Bases. "I say, 'Hooray for Art!' If the artist wants to remain in the shadows, that's fine."

My mother rapped her gavel again. "We have a motion on the floor. All in favor of a reward, raise their hands. Now all opposed."

Mom counted the votes.

"The motion is passed," she said. "A one hundred dollar reward will be offered for the identity of the shadow artist. We need a committee to be in charge of the reward."

My father groaned. "Another committee."

An Ugly Shadow

A hundred dollars! I could almost taste it. A ten-speed bike. A Walkman! A computer that did graphics! New records! Just having a hundred dollars that was all mine. Nobody would be able to tell me how to spend it. Nobody could tell me that I was wasting money.

I stayed up late that night and made a map in my notebook of where each shadow painting was located. I stared at my map. It wasn't a big area. I could walk it in about fifteen minutes.

I woke up on Saturday morning determined to win the reward money. My parents sleep late on Saturday morning, and Diana and I get our own breakfast.

When I got to the kitchen Diana was making French toast.

"Do you want some?" she asked.

"I don't have time." I poured myself some cold cereal. Her French toast looked good.

"Where are you going?" she asked.

"Out," I mumbled.

"I want to go with you."

"You can't. It's no place for a kid. I'm going to catch the shadow artist."

"Are you going to turn yourself in?" she asked.

"Very funny."

"Well, everyone thinks you're doing the paintings." Diana looked at me very slyly. "I'll tell all the kids at school that you *aren't* the shadow painter if you take me with you today."

I sighed. "Okay, it's a deal. But you keep quiet. I'm going to ask the questions."

Diana swallowed a huge piece of French toast. "So we split the reward?"

I did a double take. "How did you find out about the reward? You were asleep when we came back."

"I can read." Diana handed me the newspaper. There was an article about the shadow artist complete with pictures. The headline read: *$100 for Artist's Identity.*

"Now the entire city will be searching," I said.

"That means we better get moving," said Diana. "Oh, by the way, there's a note from Mom and Dad, and twenty dollars. They want you to do some shopping."

"Okay," I said, picking up the list. I stuffed the twenty in my pocket.

Just before leaving our building, I stopped. An envelope was shoved above our mailbox. Somebody had written LAMONT in block letters. It looked like a little kid's writing.

I grabbed the envelope. No stamp. I had a bad feeling about that envelope. I opened it. That envelope was dynamite.

"Is this your idea of a joke?" I asked.

I handed the piece of cheap white paper to Diana.

The note was signed with a crude drawing of a shadow.

"I didn't write that!" protested Diana. "I can spell. P–O–L–I–C–E."

I folded the note carefully and put it in my pocket with the twenty dollar bill. It put a whole different light on the shadow paintings. Blackmail casts an ugly shadow.

Outside, my shadow was still painted on the stoop. It gave me the creeps. I hated the person who had painted it. Did someone know about the time that I stole a bag of pretzels? What about the time I went under the subway turnstile without paying? Or the time I dropped water balloons out the window. I tried to think of what other laws I had broken.

"Who knows what evil lurks. . ." I muttered.

"Lamont, that's not funny," said Diana.

"I know," I said grimly. "Suddenly it's not funny at all."

We decided to start at Zylber's Butcher Shop. I told Diana about Mr. Zylber grabbing me at the pizza parlor.

"I wonder if he got a note too," Diana said. "I bet he thought you wrote it. No wonder he hates you."

"You're right. Last night, I never thought about blackmail. Maybe the shadow paintings are a way to mark people for blackmail."

"But why would anyone want to blackmail you?" asked Diana. "Even if you threw that water bomb, you don't have much money."

I didn't realize that Diana knew about the water bomb!

We arrived in front of the butcher shop. Saturday is Zylber's busiest day. There were limousines parked in front of the shop. A limousine could belong to an underworld kingpin. The windows of the limousines were tinted so you couldn't see inside.

Could the underworld have hired an artist to make the paintings and then send the blackmail notes? Only you'd think a Mafia kingpin would know how to spell.

"Don't move," growled a voice behind me. I turned. A big beefy man in a pinstriped suit

wearing mirrored sunglasses stood by one of the limousines. His hand was in his pocket.

I swallowed hard. All I could see was our reflection in the man's sunglasses. He kept his hand in his pocket. Did he have a gun? I tried to shove Diana behind me.

He whipped out his hand. I ducked. He brought out a tiny camera, the kind they use in spy movies.

"You two are cute. I want to take your picture against the wall next to the shadow painting."

I cringed at the word cute, but Diana gave the man her sweetest smile. "Is this going to be in the paper?" she asked.

"Shut up. Maybe he's taking my picture to show to the police," I whispered through my teeth.

"Smile!" commanded the man as he snapped our picture again. He put his camera back in his pocket and headed inside the butcher shop.

I peered in the doorway. There was a long line of customers. "It's too busy," I said. "We'll never get to talk to Mr. Zylber alone. Let's try old lady Bases. We'll come back here later."

Ms. Bases was sitting outside her shop. She had a pad of notepaper on her lap. Now that I thought about it, whenever I passed she usually had a pad on her lap. Could she be doing sketches for shadow paintings? Could my letter have come from her pad?

"Hi, Ms. Bases," said Diana. "Did you see the newspaper this morning? There was an article about the shadow paintings."

"Lousy newspaper. They didn't print a picture of *my* shadow. My shadow is much better than Zylber's."

"It's thinner," I admitted, trying to edge closer to her notepad.

"What are you doing poking around here, Lamont?" she asked. "Trying to win yourself that reward or. . . ." She looked at me suspiciously.

"Or what?" I asked.

"Or, are you more of a creep than I ever suspected?" Ms. Bases glared at me. "Get out of here, Lamont."

I was desperate. I needed to see what was written on the pad. "Ms. Bases, look," I said. "A tourist is looking at your shadow painting. Don't you want to talk to her?"

Ms. Bases would never turn away from a customer. She left her chair and put her pad down. "Hello," said Ms. Bases to her customer. "You look like a person of good taste."

"Cover me, Diana," I whispered. I bent down and fingered through the pad. It was full of numbers. I tried to figure out what they might mean.

I didn't notice that the customer had left.

"Lamont!" whispered Diana.

She was too late. Ms. Bases was standing over me. She grabbed her notebook out of my hands. "You sneaky little twerp," she hissed. "Is the Internal Revenue Service hiring pint-sized punks these days? You'd better come clean, Lamont!"

"Wait a minute, Ms. Bases, please!" I urged. "Did you get a threatening letter too?" I took out my letter and showed it to her.

Ms. Bases read it. "Was that why you were looking at my notebook? You thought I sent you such a slimy letter."

"I . . . I . . . ."

Ms. Bases pulled out a folded sheet of paper from the back of her pad. "I got one too," she said. "I thought maybe you sent it."

It was almost exactly the same as my note.

the shadow knows.
the polise will know too
if you dont come up with money.
I will call.

"Did the letter writer call you?" I asked.

"Not yet," said Ms. Bases. "I'll hang up. I've got nothing to hide." She looked at the shadow painting of herself on the wall. "It's a pity. This ruins my feelings about the painting. I loved it, but now it looks dirty to me. I can't stand looking at it when I think of the lousy creep who must have painted it."

"Can I keep your letter for a while?" I asked. "Diana and I are going to catch the lousy creep."

"Sure, you'll save me the trouble of burning it." I put Ms. Bases' note in my pocket along with my own. Some detective I was turning out to be. It was one thing to tell Ms. Bases we were going to catch the creep. All I had so far was a big fat zero.

"Where to next?" Diana asked.

I consulted my map.

"The Don't Go Down Lady."

"Oh no," groaned Diana.

"We've got to check them all out," I said.

The Don't Go Down Lady was on her corner by the subway entrance. Her shopping cart was by her side. "Hello," I said. "It was good to see you at the meeting."

"Don't go down," she answered. Her eyes looked more cloudy than usual.

"This is my sister, Diana."

She gave Diana a sideways glance. "Don't go down," she hissed.

I felt sad that she was back to saying nothing but "don't go down."

"Did you get a threatening letter?" I asked.

"DON'T GO DOWN!" she shouted.

I jumped. Diana ducked behind me.

"Don't worry," I said. "I'm going to catch the twerp who did the paintings and wrote the letter." I was sure that she had gotten a letter too.

Diana gave her a backwards glance as we left the subway stop in a hurry. "I told you we shouldn't have bothered with her," said Diana. "She's nuts."

"She isn't," I said. "When she came to the meeting, she could talk in sentences. She's just scared of something."

"Why would anyone blackmail her?" Diana asked. "She has even less money than you do."

"You're right," I said. "It doesn't make sense. It looks like the blackmailer is sending letters to everyone whose shadow was painted. It doesn't seem to matter who they are."

"Why not just do pictures of rich people?" asked Diana. "At least if you blackmail a rich person, there's a chance you'll get paid."

"You know," I said thoughtfully, "that's a very good question."

5

A Nose Job

It was still pretty early for a basketball game. On a Saturday morning, most of the players don't even wake up until noon. But Wily Will was on the court, warming up with some shadow boxing. Diana and I watched him from outside the chain link fence. His hands were fast, punching the air, pow, pow, pow.

I looked down at his shadow painting. Something bothered me about that shadow. I opened my notebook and looked down at the sketch I had made of Wily Will during the meeting.

"Look at his nose," I whispered to Diana.

"It's rude to stare."

"I mean at the nose of his shadow painting," I said.

Just then Wily Will stopped shadow boxing and came over to the fence, dribbling the basket-

34

ball. "That your girlfriend, Lamont? You robbing the cradle?"

I blushed.

"I'm Lamont's sister, Diana. I'm named after Wonder Woman."

"Wonder Woman, huh?" Wily Will sniffed.

"I call her Wonder Shrimp," I said.

"Wonder Woman was the greatest Amazon of all!" shouted Diana.

"You play basketball, Amazon?"

Diana and I went out on the court. "Hey, Wily Will, Diana doesn't have any money."

"I don't hustle little kids. Come on, I'll give you a few pointers." He flung the ball at Diana. "Shoot," he said.

She tried to make a lay-up and missed.

"Try again," said Wily Will. He bounced the ball to her.

Diana missed again.

Wily Will gave me the ball. I made my first jump shot.

Wily Will grinned at me. "Not bad for a shadow."

"Let me try again," said Diana.

Diana tried. She came close, but she missed again. "Stop looking at the ground so much," Wily Will advised.

"I can't help it," said Diana. "The shadow on

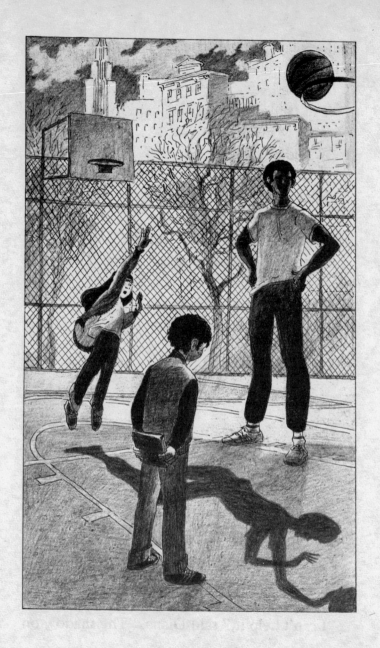

the court looks so much like you, except . . . ."

"Diana!" I shouted. "Be careful . . . uh . . . careful of where you shoot," I added quickly.

I looked down at the shadow painting. My guess was right. The artist hadn't made a mistake on any of the other paintings.

Diana made a basket. She whooped with joy. Wily Will winked at me. "Your sister's not Wonder Woman, but she's . . . ."

I stared at Wily Will's nose. I wanted to be wrong.

"What are you staring at kid?" Wily Will asked.

There was only one thing I could say. "The Shadow Nose."

"You're talking crazy," said Wily Will, but he rubbed his broken nose, and I knew that I was right.

"You're the shadow artist," I said. "Every other shadow painting was absolutely accurate, down to the bump on my nose, Zylber's fat belly, Ms. Bases' stringy legs. None of the rest of us were prettied up. But you gave yourself a nose job."

Wily Will threw the ball back at me. I stumbled back on Diana, and we both fell right on Wily Will's shadow. Wily Will under us, Wily

Will above us, we were surrounded. He glared as if he was ready to turn us into permanent shadows.

"You think you can pick up that hundred dollars on a nose," snarled Wily Will.

I picked myself up off the ground. "This painting of you is really my favorite," I said. "That way it shows you going up for a jump shot. It's the most beautiful one of them all."

"Thanks," muttered Wily Will. His hand jumped to his mouth.

"You're welcome," I said. "You're a great artist and a rotten human being."

I dusted myself off. Wily Will grabbed me by the collar. "What did you say?" His face was just inches from mine.

"You're choking me," I squawked.

Diana jumped on Wily Will's back. She clung to him like a shadow. Finally Wily Will let me go and Diana scrambled off his back. "You made those shadow paintings just to scare people," Diana shouted angrily.

"What's the chick talking about?" Wily Will asked me.

"Watch who you call a chick," warned Diana. "I'll turn you into a scrambled egg."

"Can't you shut her up?"

I shook my head. "Nobody can, but she's right anyhow. You must have sent the letters to everyone. You must have figured that everyone has a secret in their past that they want to hide."

"I'm telling you Lamont, I don't know what you're talking about."

Wily Will's eyes wouldn't let me go. I didn't know what to believe. Wily Will was a hustler on the basketball court, true. But somehow I didn't believe he was a bad guy.

I took the letters out of my pocket and showed them to him.

"What are you doing?" demanded Diana. "We need those letters for evidence. We've got to take them to the P–O–L–I–C–E."

"I know how to spell, girlie."

Diana started to open her mouth, but something about Wily Will's expression made her close it again. Will crushed one letter in his hand. "Where did you get this?"

"It was on top of our mailbox this morning. It wasn't sent through the mails."

"You wrote those letters," said Diana. "You're the shadow artist."

I shook my head. "I don't think you wrote them, Wily Will. I think you did the paintings, but you didn't write the letters."

"You're crazy, Lamont," said Diana. "He's got you conned."

"Look at the shadow paintings," I said, pointing down to the beautiful painting of Wily Will on the court. "They're perfect. Do you think the same person who did the paintings on the sidewalks would make those splotches on the letters?"

Wily Will bounced the ball up and down on his painted shadow. "You're right, Lamont. I did the paintings on the street, but I never sent *anybody* any letters. I wouldn't have done that. I only painted people I liked. I've always loved to draw, all my life, but I never thought I could make any money at it. I dropped out of school. I can't get a job, so I hustle basketball games. But no crime. I've stayed clean. Then one day, I caught sight of my shadow when I was going for a lay-up. It looked beautiful to me. I started painting shadows on the street. It was my secret life. But I don't *blackmail!*"

"But if you didn't send the letters, who did?" Diana asked.

"That's what we've got to find out," I said.

P·O·L·I·S·E

"Thanks." Wily Will put his big hands on my shoulders. "Thanks for believing me."

"Forget it," I said. "Just because I believe you, doesn't mean you're in the clear. Does anybody else know you're the shadow artist?"

Wily Will shook his head. "No. I made sketches of the paintings, but I kept them hidden in my room at the YMCA, the one I share with Swivel Hips. I've always been quick with my hands, in paintings just like in basketball. I do the paintings *real* fast."

Just then Swivel Hips George came onto the court. "Hey, Wily Will, you playing with girl shadows now?" he asked.

"I'm not a shadow," snapped Diana.

"Hey, be cool, George," said Wily Will. "These kids here are my friends."

I felt proud that Wily Will would call me his friend. Swivel Hips George didn't seem to like it. He gave Diana and me a dirty look. "Hand me that ball," he said.

Diana dribbled the ball in front of her. She made no move to pass it.

"Did you hear me?" asked Swivel Hips.

Suddenly I had an idea. "Hey, Swivel Hips," I said. "I bet Wily Will that he couldn't spell police, and I won five dollars."

"You won five dollars off Wily Will? A little pipsqueak like you?"

Wily Will spread out his huge hands. He shrugged. "The kid made a bet and he won."

"Ha," snorted Swivel Hips.

"I'll give you a chance to win it back for Wily Will. I'll bet you ten bucks you can't spell police."

"Ha. I can spell police. I can *smell* police. I just don't *like* police. Ten bucks isn't enough."

"Twenty bucks says you can't." My stomach was doing somersaults. I had twenty dollars in my pocket, but it was the money Mom and Dad gave me to do the weekend food shopping. If I lost it, I would be in big, big trouble.

Swivel Hips stopped dribbling. "What's the con, kid? You think I'm stupid or something?"

"I just don't think you can spell police."

Swivel Hips George swiveled away. He made a lay-up. "Kid, I'm not going to bite."

"Okay," I said. "I'll give you odds. Ten to one."

"Ha, it's a sucker bet."

"Look, I'll make it twenty to one."

"Lamont," said Diana. "Can I talk to you?" She grabbed my arm and half dragged me over to the fence. "Lamont, are you crazy? Even I know that's a stupid bet. Do you know that means you have to pay four hundred dollars if you lose? Four hundred dollars! What are you going to do?"

"I'm not going to lose," I said.

Wily Will came over to us. "Lamont, do you know what you're doing?"

"I'm on a roll," I said.

Wily Will and Diana exchanged anxious glances. "If you ask me," said Diana, "he's gone bonkers."

"Easiest bucks I'll ever earn," sneered Swivel Hips. "P–O–L. . . ."

I held my breath. If I was wrong, I was sunk deeper than the Titanic. I looked across the street and my stomach did a triple somersault. A police car was parked right in front of the playground. The word POLICE was there in big blue letters. All Swivel Hips had to do was look across

the street, and all that money would fly away.

Diana followed my eyes. Casually she skipped to the far side of the playground, away from the street. Swivel Hips kept his eyes on her. "That girl is ruining my concentration," he said.

"Diana, stand still," I ordered, thankful she'd been smart enough to keep Swivel Hips from looking at the police car.

"Go on, Swivel Hips," said Wily Will. "Finish the word."

"P–O–L–I–S–E."

"Just like you spelled it on the blackmail notes you've been writing!" I shouted.

"Ha," snorted Swivel Hips. "Since when is it a crime to misspell a word? You gonna call the police?"

"We just might do that," I said. "Blackmail is against the law."

Wily Will glowered at Swivel Hips. "You sent those stupid letters to everyone except *me* cause you knew I'd recognize your handwriting."

"You recognized his handwriting?" I asked.

Wily Will nodded. "As soon as I saw it. You don't think I'd have let you really risk four hundred dollars."

"I was scared," I admitted. But I realized that you were the only one who didn't get a note. It had to be Swivel Hips. Since you were room-mates, he knew you'd guess he was sending the notes."

"Now, wait a minute, Will," Swivel Hips pleaded. "No need to get all hot and bothered. I would have given you a cut. Seeing those shadows made me think. I figured everyone had something to hide. Then, when you said Lamont was The Shadow, I got a great idea. I just dropped off my little notes after you did the paintings. I figured the kid would be blamed."

Wily Will looked as if he wanted to kill Swivel Hips. "You lousy creep. I liked those people I drew. I only joked about Lamont's name because I didn't want anyone to guess it was me. Now you've ruined everything." He lunged for Swivel Hips.

"Hold it, Wily Will," I said.

"Right," said Diana, running over to the police car. "Help!" she shouted. "P–O–L–I–C–E!"

The Real Nose

We all went to the police station. It was a madhouse. The police, of course, knew all about the shadow paintings. They even knew about the blackmail. Mr. Zylber had taken his note to them. But it took them a long time to understand that there were two shadows. The artist and the creep!

The police called all the people who had received notes and asked them to come to the station. They also called my mom and dad.

Swivel Hips called a lawyer.

"Some friend," snorted Wily Will as he watched Swivel Hips make his phone call. We were sitting on a bench in the precinct house. Wily Will was slumped on the bench. He looked more sad than mad.

"I'm sorry it turned out to be your friend," I said.

"He's no friend," said Wily Will. "And don't waste your time feeling sorry about Swivel Hips. He probably won't stay in jail very long, if at all."

"It's not Swivel Hips I'm worried about," I said. "It's you."

"Yeah, what about you, Wily Will?" asked Diana. "What are you going to do now?"

Wily Will shrugged. "I guess I'll go back to the playground and hustle up a game." Wily Will rubbed his nose. "To think, all because of a nose. I was just too vain to paint my nose the way it is. Well, you taught me a lesson, Lamont. I'm going to keep my paintings in a deep shadow from now on. . . ."

I was mad. Wily Will's talent was too good to stay in a closet.

Just then my parents came bursting into the precinct house.

"Lamont!" cried my mother. "What's wrong?"

"Nothing. Calm down. I found out who the shadow artist is," I said.

"In the police station?" asked my father.

"No, on the basketball court. Mom and Dad,

I want you to meet the best artist on the street, Will . . ." I paused. I realized I never knew Wily Will's last name.

"Will Harris," mumbled Wily Will.

My father held out his hand. "Pleased to meet you Will. I've been admiring your art every time I leave my front door. It sort of stares me in the face. You've got a lot of talent."

"And Dad's a professional artist," said Diana proudly.

Wily Will looked embarrassed.

"Who's the artist?" demanded Ms. Bases. She was followed by Mr. Zylber. The Don't Go Down Lady stood shyly in the corner.

"I'm no artist," said Wily Will softly.

I introduced Wily Will to everybody. The police had already explained to them that the blackmail letters had not come from the shadow artist and that the blackmailer was in custody.

"You!" said Ms. Bases. "I've seen you on the basketball court. What are you wasting your time playing basketball for?"

"Good question," said my father.

Wily Will looked as if he wanted to disappear.

"Hey," piped up Diana. "We win the reward! We found the shadow artist."

"That's right," said my mother. "Lamont, I guess you and Diana have won the reward."

"I won it," I argued. "I won it by a nose."

Diana squinched up her face. "But I helped."

I sighed. "You did," I admitted. I looked over in the corner. My father was in deep conversation with Wily Will. I wondered what they were talking about.

"Diana, I've got an idea," I said.

"Oh no," warned Diana. "Your ideas usually end up getting us in trouble."

"This one won't," I promised. "It's a great way we can share the reward."

"I already know a great way. You get fifty bucks, and I get fifty bucks."

"No, this is better." I whispered my idea in Diana's ear.

At first she didn't like it, but the more she heard, the better it sounded to her. Finally, she nodded her head. "Okay," she whispered back. "But we share it, remember."

I agreed.

"What's up?" asked my mom.

I cleared my throat. "I have an announcement," I said. "As you know, Diana and I have just won a hundred dollars. We want to buy a painting. In fact, we want your painting, Wily Will. We would like you to put our favorite shadow painting on canvas, the one of you going for a lay-up."

"Right," said Diana. "Because, I'm going to grow up to be a great basketball player, and your painting will inspire me."

For a wonder shrimp, Diana's got great dreams.

Wily Will stared at us. "You'd pay a hundred dollars just for a painting?"

My father smiled. "That's what I was talking to you about. Actually I think Lamont and Diana are making a good investment. If you have the guts to stick with painting, I think you could go far. You sure have the raw talent for it."

Ms. Bases practically sprang forward. "I have to admit that your shadow paintings have attracted a number of tourists. I have a feeling that if I carried some of your paintings in my shop, I might be able to sell them. We'll have to talk about commissions, of course."

Wily Will smiled. He and Ms. Bases had a lot in common. They both liked a good hustle.

The Don't Go Down Lady motioned to me. She whispered in my ear.

"Wily Will," I said. "This lady would like you to sign her painting by the subway entrance."

Wily Will nodded gravely. "I'd be glad to," he said.

"But our painting should come first," said Diana. "We asked first."

"And we want you to correct the nose," I added. "We want the real Wily Will's nose."

"Right," said Wily Will. He laughed. I had never seen Wily Will look so happy. "Well, it looks like I might not be having too much time for basketball these days."

My father put his arm around Will's shoulder. "Why don't you come around to my studio and we'll have a long talk."

"Thanks," said Will. "I'd like it."

We walked out of the precinct house. Dad and Will were deep in conversation. Mom was talking to Ms. Bases. Diana and I trailed behind.

"It's weird," she said.

"What's weird?" I asked.

"We just caught a creepy blackmailer and already everyone has forgotten about him. All anybody cares about is Wily Will and his art."

"It seems right," I said. "There will always be lots of creeps like Swivel Hips around, but there aren't many Wily Wills in the world."

"There aren't many Lamont Shapiros in the world either," said Diana. "Where would the shadow artist be without the original Shadow!" She flashed me a smile.

For a wonder shrimp, Diana isn't all bad. In fact, sometimes she lives up to her name. Sometimes I do too. We make a good pair.